Jail House Wifey

BY: ANGELINA WILSON

Publishers address:
Niagara Falls, NY. 14305

Email: mrs.author@myself.com
Facebook.com/Authroess Angelina Wilson
Instagram.com/mrs._author2019

ACKNOWLEDGMENTS

*F*irst and foremost, I would like to thank God himself for blessing me! Who would have thought I'd make it this far? This is my first book, my first novella. But I promise it won't be the last. I want to thank each person who picks up a copy of my first book.

Without support from each of you, none of this would be possible. Thank you!

I want to thank my mother Yvonne Johnson, who is also my hero and my Queen. You have always believed in me, even when I didn't believe in myself. You told me to keep pushing and that I did. I love you, mom.

To my fiance, Nick Levick. Thank you for always having an ear, and for pushing me to write. You gave me positive and negative feedback, which allowed me to improve as a writer. I love you and they can't hold you forever. FREE YOU!

To my big brother James Wilson and my big sister Chenita Johnson, I love you both.

To my two little girls, mommy loves you. You both are the many reasons why I go so hard.

Tara Ezell, thank you so much for this opportunity, without your classes I probably wouldn't have completed this book. Thank you, you are appreciated!

NIAGARA FALLS, NY. Stand up!! Shout out to everyone in the 716, you all are appreciated. The support has been phenomenal. Thank you!

PROLOGUE

*S*itting in a crowded courtroom was the last place I wanted to be. But being the down ass chick I am, I felt I had no other choice. This was not my first time being in this unfortunate situation, and it never gets any easier.

I'm Angela Weston, 20 years old with a heart of gold. Many say I'm mature for my age. I handle my business and I mind my business. I have the looks of a model, if I wasn't tied up with Trey, I probably would have been. I'm 5'8," with long thick legs. My deep chocolate dark-skin was the color of a milk chocolate candy bar. My alluring figure caught the attention of many, which made Trey keep me right by his side. Attention was not something I was fond of, however, whenever I entered a room all eyes were on me. Many thought I was from the Islands because of my distinct accent and exotic looks. Nonetheless, I was fully black with some percentage of Indian in my blood. I don't mean to toot my own horn, but I'm far from your average chick.

On the flip side, I was always in and out of court for my man. I must say, I'm the true definition of a ride or die chick. Trey is my world as I am his. However, the commissary, collect calls, and visits were taking their toll on me. I didn't complain though, since I knew what trey was into when we met four years ago. No matter what, I vowed to always hold him down.

Court hadn't started yet, I couldn't keep still; I began fidgeting with my fingers and squirming on the hard bench. All I could do is think of what the Judge might hand down to my already two times convicted felon.

Thinking back years ago when I first met Trey, as soon as we locked eyes I fell in love with him. I guess the saying opposites attract was true. He was 5'5" and stocky. His high yellow skin complexion had people thinking he was Puerto Rican; he wasn't.

I was his supermodel and he was my superman, I loved every bit of him. Even though Trey was on the short side, people respected him. His attitude made up for what he lacked in height. He was a known drug lord, so no one was stupid enough to test his gangster. Everyone knew what he was capable of, he was never afraid to let his guns bust.

"All rise." The court officer snapped me out of my trance, I felt my stomach twist in knots as the county sheriff escorted Trey out in handcuffs. I had to smile just a little bit. Although the circumstances were brutal, he was looking good; his fade was fresh, his sneakers were fresh, and he looked like he just got a fresh trim. He looked over at me for a brief moment, he smiled and mouthed "I love you."

Trey had been locked up for eight months now, of course, I was being faithful. I was getting worked up just looking at him, imagining his face between my thighs. The last time we had sex played in my head, and that vision alone set off fireworks between my legs.

"Please be seated," snapped me back to the harsh reality as the court officer looked at me like I was crazy. I was standing there daydreaming about my man, fuck them I thought to myself while taking a seat. Trey's mom looked at me puzzled, I tapped her shoulder letting her know I was fine.

Inmate after inmate was called, the Judge had no mercy on them.

"No bail," was all I heard the Judge telling the inmates. As much as I wanted to cry, fearing the same would happen with Trey, I held my composure and crossed my fingers.

The court secretary finally called out his name, "Trey Isaac Godfrey."

He stood up, with his hands cuffed in front of him.
"Two counts for possession of a controlled substance, one count for resisting arresting, and reckless driving." As the clerk went on with more and more charges, the Judge shook his head in disgust. My nerves were taking over, I toyed with my fingers and shook my right leg anxiously.

Trey's lawyer stood up in his defense. He was one of the best-paid lawyers in town; he better pull some damn strings. Before court, I dropped him off an additional $25,000. That was on top of the thousands I already paid him months ago, my man better come the fuck home.

"Is there something you would like to say, Mr. Rivers?" The judge shifted his attention to Trey's lawyer. "Yes, your Honor. My client was pulled over without probable cause, he has lost eight months of his life due to driving while black. I would like for my client to be released immediately, due to racial profiling." Mr. Rivers presented his evidence and the Judge looked it over for a brief moment. "So, Mr. Godfrey was pulled over as it says here in the report, with no explanation as to why. His car was searched, and drugs were seized." Unfortunately, this illegal stop and search were unconstitutional. Therefore, I have no other choice but to release Mr. Godfrey. All charges dismissed," the judge concluded while banging his gavel. The courtroom erupted with cheer! The arresting officers were disgusted as they thought they had finally caught the man who had been terrorizing their city.

After hearing the verdict, I jumped up and hugged Trey's Mom. We both cried tears of joy. It was a must to have people in high places on your payroll when you're in the type of business Trey is in. But, even people in high places can get jealous of your power and try to bring you down. As Trey was escorted out by the officers, a pair of hateful eyes watched him from the back of the courtroom. Surprisingly, no one noticed the wandering eyes including me. If I would have been watching my surroundings, I would have seen the obvious hate. It could all be too late for Trey when those same eyes become the reason his empire would begin to slowly tumble down.

TABLE OF CONTENTS

CHAPTER 1

ANGELA

Two Years Later:

"*R*unning around with Trey got me tired as hell, Peaches. I ain't tryna go to nobody's club tonight, just because your no good ass niggas let you run with the wind, don't mean I can join you. Trey ain't havin' that anyhow. You also know I'm pregnant and I still have yet to tell Trey." I tried to explain to my friend of 10 years. Peaches and I, have been friends longer than I've been with Trey. We went from grade school enemies to high school besties. Peaches were more of the outgoing, outspoken type. I on the other hand was shy and quiet. Peaches and I are the same height. She has long brownish colored hair, hazel eyes, and on the heavy side. She carried her weight well though. Ghetto fabulous is exactly what she is, always rocking big hoop earrings and shorts that were two sizes too small, with her belly hanging over them. Let her tell it, she looks the bomb.

"Girl why are you always up under Trey's ass? Let that boy do that shit alone, you ain't no hustler's wife,"

Peaches yelled in my ear on the opposite end of the phone.

"I may not be his wife but I damn sure play the position," I barked back.

"Well, when you get a ring holla at me. Until then I'll be shaking my ass on the dance floor thotin' it out." Being the good friend that I was, I just ignored Peaches' comment. Marvin, who has been Peaches' boyfriend for about four years, was a dog himself. He had too many bitches to try and keep up with what Peaches was doing, or should I say who she was doing. They had an apartment together but he was gone so much that Peaches had to do things to occupy her time.

"Pop! Pop! Pop!"

Three gunshots went off as I ducked down, not knowing where they were coming from. I've been sitting outside Trey's stash house for about thirty minutes, sitting in our 2014 white on white Escalade. My heart pounded rapidly since I knew he was still inside. I pulled out my Glock 36 and exited the truck. Taking two steps, I saw the front door burst open and Trey run out.
"Yo Ang! Get in the V, man. Niggas tried to take me out; I'm hit. We gotta make moves before 12 come, Ma." I jumped back in the truck nervous as hell, I didn't know where he was hit. I had to stay focused, knowing Trey

had about 3 pounds of weight in the back seat, on top of the money he just collected. The last thing we needed was to get pulled over.

"Hey, Baby, you ok?" I asked Trey, trying to keep him awake and talking. Blood seeped from his wounds as he sat there in excruciating pain. "Yeah, I'm good. Just hit the stash house on Kingston and drop this load off so I can get to the hospital," Trey mumbled in agony.

Making sure to obey all traffic signs and staying at the required speed limit, we finally arrived at the stash house. I put my Glock in my secret compartment as I unloaded the bags from the back and stashed them at his spot. As I ran back towards the truck, Trey was slumped over.

"Baby wake up! Don't you quit on me T! You're strong, baby." I tried not to bug out knowing Trey needed medical attention like yesterday, I calmed myself and hopped back in the driver's seat. Putting on the hazard lights, I flew through traffic. We were only about 5 minutes away from the hospital.

I made it there in record time and pulled right up to the front, honking my horn non-stop.

"Trey, Baby we here. You're going to make it baby, I promise!" I jumped out of the truck, and the nurses brought over a stretcher. He's been shot. I screamed, "Somebody please help him."

Trey lay lifeless on the stretcher as they worked on him while rushing him into the back. I followed them eagerly, but the nurse stopped me and said they needed to take him right to the operating table; I wasn't allowed back.

"We're going to lose him, we have to find out where all this blood is coming from," I heard the nurse say as the doors closed shut right in my face. I couldn't lose Trey, he was all I had. I couldn't hold my composure any longer and burst into tears. Remembering the truck was parked illegally, I got my breathing under control and tried to calm myself as I walked outside. As soon as I got in the truck, I felt my phone vibrating on the floor. It was Peaches, so I answered.

"Yo, what the fuck is going on Ang? I heard the gunshots and then the phone went blank. You alright?"

"No! I'm not ok, Peach. Trey was shot, they shot my fuckin' baby."

"Oh damn. I'm so sorry, I'm going to hit up Marvin and we will be down there. Stay strong, girl. I'll be there real soon."

I hung up with Peaches and just cried uncontrollably as reality set in that Trey could be dying back there, and there was nothing I could do about it.

CHAPTER 2
TREY

Guns started bustin' and bullets started flying, all I knew was I had to get out of Dodge. So, I started running and shooting my way out. I saw shadows but no faces and niggas aiming their guns at me. I'm outnumbered but my guns bust just like theirs, so I did what any real nigga would do; try to survive. I was so close to the door where I could escape the madness, until I felt a hot sensation consume my body. I ain't never been shot before, but I knew I was hit, that shit was burning like a mothafucka. As I reached for the door, I heard a few shots.

"Pop! Pop!"

Before the darkness devoured me, I heard a familiar voice say, "You can't be the king forever," as I took my last breath.

My eyes popped open and a few teary eyes stared back at me. I didn't know where the hell I was, but I saw Angela first; then my Moms, my right-hand man Marv, and Peaches. Balloons and flowers filled the room as I tried to move, but I couldn't. I tried to talk but nothing would come out. My throat felt dry as hell and it felt like something was poking me in my dick. Angela ran to my bed with tears in her eyes. "I'm so glad you're awake, T! Oh my God! I can't believe you're finally awake," she cried frantically. Angela ran out of the room and came back in with a short white nurse. I looked at the nurse and pointed to my mouth.

"Yes, Honey, I know it's very irritating. However, those tubes kept you breathing when you were in a coma." The nurse began to fill me in, she caught me off guard as she spoke.

Did she say a fuckin' coma? I thought to myself. I couldn't believe what I was hearing. I wasn't dreaming then. This shit was real. Was I shot? Was I in a car accident? Man, I was about to bug the fuck out if somebody didn't tell me what was going on, I thought as my mind started racing. Angela must have seen the worried expression on my face, she was back at my bedside after the nurse left out.

"Trey, I know you don't know what the hell is going on, but you have been in a coma and we didn't think you would come out of it. You were shot. Right now, we have to wait for the anesthesiologist, it's their job to take all these tubes out."

I let Angela fill me in without interrupting, just nodding my head each time her beautiful self looked at me.

"Now like the nurse said, the one in your mouth helped you breathe; you have one in your penis, of course, that was to help you use the bathroom." It felt good hearing my wifey's voice, but I still didn't know what led up to the coma.

All I could do was look at my girl dumbfounded. Looking up to the ceiling in deeps thoughts, I didn't know what the fuck was going on or who would want to take me out. I'm the mothafucking king of NYC and mothafuckaz tried to bury me. Why though? I feed my team, I don't shit on anybody and everybody eats equal. It had to be one of them jealous cats from Jersey, who felt like I was muscling them out of some of their territory. But that's just the game, you either get it or somebody else was going to and I happened to have the weight and the workers to take over a little section in Jersey. I laid in the hospital bed thinking of all of my enemies, wondering who the snake was that I allowed getting close to me. My thoughts were interrupted, making me a little more flustered.

A tall frail man, who I assumed was the doctor entered my room causing me to snap back to the current situation. He asked everyone to leave the room, he needed to remove the tubes and check out my vitals.

"Mr. Godfrey, I'm doctor Ross. I've been in and out of this room since you came in a month ago."

A month? I asked in disbelief.

Yes, the doctor continued while shaking his head. "You have been in a coma for almost a month. You were shot three times. Once in the shoulder and twice in the chest. We were able to remove the bullet from the shoulder. The other bullet entered through the front of your chest and exited out you're back, missing all major arteries. Unfortunately, there is still a bullet lodged close to your heart. If we would have removed it, you would have bled to death. You're a very lucky man, if the bullet was an inch closer, you would have died instantly."

I had to take all this shit in. I sat there staring at the doc. I was zoned out, whatever he was saying went in one ear and out the other. I was still trying to grasp the fact, that niggas wanted me dead.

Somebody was trying to take me out. In all my years of hustling, I was never a target. It was fucked up that my memory was gone, I would have to ask Angela to fill me in on where I was and who I was with. I thought I was dreaming but this shit is real. Once I start to piece the puzzle together, a war would be the only option. I couldn't let this shit ride. Niggas would think I'm weak, and I wasn't going to be labeled as a bitch nigga. This is my fuckin' city. I made niggas and put niggas on. My name is Trey mothafuckin Godfrey! I lay down for nobody and when I get up outta here, I'm shedding all kinds of blood.

The doctor told me all my vitals were good, they would keep me for observation and then release me in a couple of weeks.

My family came back to my room, my right-hand Marvin didn't say two words to me. I noticed when I first opened my eyes, our eyes locked and instead of seeing my man, I saw a nigga with larceny in his eyes.

Marvin must have felt my uneasiness, he walked over to me and shook my hand.

"I'm glad to see you decided to come back to the real world." I nodded at him to acknowledge him, I still couldn't speak above a whisper.

Before he turned and walked out of my room, he looked back at me and said, "You gotta take it easy, Bro; you can't be king forever." That shit sounded so familiar but I couldn't place it just yet. Sooner than later everything would start falling into place, the streets were always talking. I knew I still had a bullet in me, but it wouldn't stop me from putting a bullet in someone else.

CHAPTER 3

ANGELA

*T*his month has been nothing but pure hell for me. With Trey being in the hospital, I had to take on his responsibilities to keep our empire from falling. Delivering packages up and down the I-90, collecting his money, making visits, and making sure shit was running properly, was draining. On top of all that, I had to make sure his workers were handing in the money. Every night they dropped off the money to me, re-up and do it all again the following night. I didn't have any problems with his workers; most of them were loyal to Trey. There were always a few though, in this case, there were two of them. A young cat named Clean and Trey's right hand, Marvin. Clean just wanted to question my authority, so I had to be a boss bitch and put the Lil nigga back in his place, which was easy. Now Marvin, on the other hand, wanted to try to test me on a different level.

Walking back to my car after dropping off the work to the corner boys on Smithson street, my feet were killing me. I presented myself as the wifey, to a boss. Wearing an army green two-piece pantsuit, with army fatigue thigh boots, I was on shit!

As I crossed the street, Marvin rolled up beside me. His ride was flashy, everyone knew when he was coming. Not the smarter move, especially when he didn't have a job. The cops harass black folks in expensive shit, he didn't have paperwork like us. Marvin rolled the window down while parking in the middle of the street.

"Angela, let me holla at you right quick," his voice slurred and his eyes were low. He was high for sure.

"What's up?" I was already annoyed, my feet were hurting and I wanted to sit down. I knew it sounded like I had an attitude, and I did.

"Come on Angela, hop in the V and let's take a spin right quick," he offered.

"Nah, I'm good. Whatever you need to say, can be said with me standing right here. I need to get home and prepare for my man to be released tomorrow. I don't have time for you or yo shit."

"See bitch, that's your problem now, you got a smart ass mouth. If your body wasn't banging, Trey would have been left ya stuck-up ass," Marvin shot back as he opened his door to exit his car. He was trying to intimidate me, with his solid frame and deep voice.

"Boy, fuck you. You wish you were half the man Trey is. You mad you can't have me, huh? I'm his for life bitch, get over it." I walked away and headed towards my truck, unlocking my doors while doing so. I attempted to get back in my truck, not realizing Marvin was right behind me.

"All that ass you got," he mumbled as he smacked my ass hard as hell. I turned around quickly and smacked him across his face, busting his bottom lip. I hopped in my truck and locked the doors, I was pissed that he even touched me. As I sped off, I looked out my rearview mirror and saw Marvin still standing there, an evil grin on his face and blood dripping from his mouth.

I tried to shake what just happened, I had to take care of some shit. Before I went home, I stopped and stashed the money at the stash house. I knew the rules of the game, and Trey would kill me for bringing that kind of bread to our home.

Trey would be released tomorrow, I had everything prepared so that he could be as comfortable as possible. As I was pulling into our driveway, a feeling of uneasiness overwhelmed me. Something didn't feel right. I stayed strapped, that gave me some comfort. I took my Glock out of my secret compartment and got out of my truck. I think the situation with Marvin got me shook up a little bit, I never had problems at my home. Then again, Trey wasn't home either.

Walking in the house, I sat my belongings down and headed for the shower. It wasn't until I started walking that I saw a shadow on the wall. My body tensed, but I made moves. My gun was in my purse by the door, so I was fucked. I ran full speed to the kitchen to grab a knife, a heavy kick in my back caused me to drop to my knees. I didn't have the chance to stand before I felt strong hands around my neck. I was being lifted off the floor, like a rag doll. I gasped for air while clawing at the person's hands.

"You want to be a down ass bitch, huh?" The unknown voice said, taunting me while his grip tightened around my neck. It was dark in my house; all the lights were off so I couldn't see. I was too busy kicking trying to do whatever I could to get free. I started to feel myself losing consciousness, little black dots were the only things visible. Before I felt myself giving up, I was dropped to the floor and kicked in my stomach three times.

"You can be touched bitch, so remember that. Just like yo' nigga was touched," the unknown man threatened before dipping out the front door.

Pain immediately shot up my stomach, it felt like my insides were being squashed. I cried as blood formed under me, the pain was unbearable, all I could do is curl up in a ball as I lay in a pool of my own blood.

How could this be happening? All I wanted to do was make Trey happy. When he came home tomorrow, I had planned to tell him we were expecting a baby. I had to be almost 2 months along. I'd only found out a week before he had been shot. I knew with the pain in my stomach and the amount of blood I lost, that our baby was gone. We wouldn't be picking out names and decorating the other empty room. We had a security system and someone was able to bypass it without the alarms going off. I didn't see how that was possible when we were supposed to have the best. It had to be some grimy shit going on, somebody set this shit up. It was now my time to become the most treacherous bitch in the city. When you fuck with a made nigga, it would always be some shit, but the family was supposed to be off-limits. If the message wasn't for Trey, somebody was taking shots at me. I was going hard these past few weeks and probably hurt a bitch niggas ego. I had no other option but to wipe my tears and lace the fuck up. When Trey recovers, shit won't be too pretty. It would only be a matter of time before the streets start talking, when I find out who the intruder was and who sent them, it would be me putting bullets throughout their fucking body.

CHAPTER 4
TREY

*G*etting released from the hospital was the best feeling in the world. They wheeled me out in a wheelchair since that's the hospital procedures, I didn't need it though. I felt like a new person, ready to raise hell in these streets. After going through rehab to regain balance, I was good. I was ready to take on whatever, whoever and whenever. My Moms came to pick me up alone, she said Angela had a doctor's appointment. I just wanted to see my boo.

Some of my memory was starting to come back a little at a time, however, I was still lost about the night I was shot. We pulled up to the house and I got out my Mom's BMW. As soon as I opened the door I heard, "Welcome home!"

They planned a surprise welcome home party for me, they had a nigga blushing and shit. All my aunts, uncles, cousins, and street niggas were present. I was an only child, so it felt good to see everyone showing love for me. An hour into the get-together, Angela finally came in, and damn my baby was looking good. It looked like she dropped a couple of pounds since the last time I saw her. Her smile alone melted my heart.

"Hey, baby! Sorry, I'm late. I had a doctor's appointment," Angela whispered in my ear while kissing me. I tried to read her body language, she was sounding somewhat down.

"It's all good baby. You with daddy now and that's all that matters," I told her while grabbing her ass. She was rocking a white and pink outfit that hugged her body in all the right places, I ain't had my dick sucked or been up in no pussy since this incident took place, I was ready to tell everybody to leave so I could beat my wifey pussy up. As I thought about it, I hope my stroke game was still good. I looked down there now and then to make sure my guy hadn't shrunk.

We enjoyed the rest of the party until around ten at night. Everybody started to leave and I wasn't the slightest bit disappointed. I thanked everyone for coming and locked up. Angela seemed distant for some reason, I wanted to change that and show her how much I appreciated her. Knowing she was holding shit down for me made me love her even more. My dick jumped slightly just thinking about her, yeah I still got it I thought to myself. "Come here, baby girl!" I called Angela over and started caressing her body; I began to unbutton her shirt, and lick her nipples. Angela started fidgeting, and I was thinking to myself, "I still got this shit." After a few seconds of sucking on her nipples, she stopped.

"T baby, I'm on my period."

"Girl, we fucked on your period before. Stop acting all shy. My anaconda still works, I ate them bullets."

Angela burst into tears. I wasn't expecting that, all I could do was hold her. Maybe she was just stressed out, or me talking about getting shot made her emotional. Whatever the reason was, I hated to see her cry. I held my lady and rocked her while playing in her hair, she loved that shit.

"Trey, I can't lie to you. I didn't want to stress you because you just got out of the hospital. But I was at the doctor's today because I had a miscarriage," Angela grumbled as the tears continued to flow.

"Damn baby, I'm sorry you've been going through this shit since I've been down, but I'm good now we can work on another baby. We ain't got nothing but time."

"Trey, somebody got past our security system somehow last night. I was attacked in our own house. Whoever he was kicked me repeatedly in my stomach and I lost our baby." Angela cried uncontrollably. I just held her in my arms with tears in my eyes, and death on my mind.

Niggas was sending for my girl now. I wasn't having that shit. I couldn't believe I failed to protect her and our unborn child. My heart was hurting knowing Angela went through that, she went through it alone and I wasn't there to hold her down.

I was going to get all my street soldiers lined up and have an emergency meeting first thing in the morning. Word spreads on the streets quickly, and I wanted everybody to keep their ears open so I could find the bitch nigga responsible for hurting my lady. She wasn't just my lady she was one of the realest niggas on my team; my future wife. If a muthafucka thought they could touch her, they didn't respect me. I was about to do some serious damage to the streets of New York. I didn't care who got in my way, bullets didn't have names for a reason.

Angela fell asleep on my chest, but I was still up thinking and plotting. As I played out the events for the day, I realized my main man didn't show up today. Marvin wasn't at the party. He had to know I was getting out today and he didn't even check on a nigga. I paged him "911," after five minutes he paged me back "000," meaning he was busy. I was starting to grow real suspicious of that nigga, something has been off with him lately. Instead of tripping, I hit my Lil man, Thug up. He's been with me for a minute and I trusted him to the fullest. I told him to get the word out that we had an emergency meeting tomorrow and everybody needed to be there. After hanging up the phone with Thug, I went and laid next to Angela. Her phone was going off, so I looked into it. Peaches, Poppin shit as always, was the first text I saw; the next message was coming from a blocked number.

The text message read:

"Watch your back in these streets. These streets ain't made for bitches."

Angela must have been in this shit hard when I was down, My baby was riding with me and I would die before I let anybody threaten her life. This message and the attack had to be connected, and I would find out sooner than later. I had to get some rest so I could focus tomorrow. I didn't need my thoughts fuckin my actions up, I was smarter than that. My pops used to say, "A man who acts without thinking is a foolish man."
I was far from foolish. I had a few strikes against me with the law, but I would risk it all without question. Somebody was about to feel my wrath. Since mothafuckas wanted to play with my family, I was putting little babies to sleep. That's on my dead seed!

CHAPTER 5
ANGELA

---

*R*iding the town with Peaches, Tupac's "White Man's World," blasting through the speakers had me in a zone. I've been cooped up in the house for about a week now, and Trey kept begging me to get up and go get some air. I don't fuck with too many of these jealous ass New York bitches, so I called up my girl Peaches and she didn't hesitate to come scoop me.

After losing the baby, I fell into depression. I felt bad since Trey was the one suffering from neglect, I hadn't had sex with him in weeks.

Today would be the day that I straightened my crown and sat back on the throne. I couldn't let this shit get the best of me; I was a made nigga's women.

As we were riding and blowing on some gas, I asked Peaches to stop at Victoria's Secret. I needed to grab something sexy to wear for Trey tonight.

"Girl, this is supposed to be our time to catch up since you went MIA on me," Peaches snarled, with a twisted facial expression.

"Peach, I'm just going to be a few minutes. I know we haven't been hanging like that, but you know I've been going through some shit." Of course, she couldn't resist my spoiled ass, I always got what I wanted.

Peaches and I exited her Toyota Camry and headed inside the mall. I was rocking a brown mini skirt, a brown and gold halter top, and gold lace-up sandals, showing off my little cute feet. My hair was slicked back in a bun, showing off my cute face. Whenever I left the house no matter how I was feeling, I had to be on point. When your man is the HNIC you have to play your position correctly. I knew Trey wasn't going anywhere, but I still had to be on point as his wifey.

It didn't take me long to find a red two-piece lingerie set and some matching heels to go with it. After I paid for my items we exited the store and headed to the Food Court to get a bite to eat. I wanted to let Peaches know about her dog ass nigga, but her ass didn't care anyhow, so I left it alone.

We decided on Auntie Anne's, then made our way over to the tables. Peaches tapped me on my shoulder and pointed in the direction of a group of bitches, they glared at us with jealousy in their eyes. Out of the group of six, I knew at least three of the chicks from around the way.

"What the fuck y'all looking at," Peaches yelled. One of the girls who goes by Diamond stuck up her middle finger, that's all it took for Peaches ghetto ass to get rowdy. Peaches made her way towards the chicks and I followed, knowing damn well if some shit was gone pop off I had her back. Even though we were outnumbered we stood our ground, Peaches wasn't scared to fight and neither was I.

"Y'all bitches got an issue or something?" "Do we look that good that y'all bitches gotta stare at us like y'all want these problems?"

Peaches addressed the entire group, but only Diamond spoke up.

"First of all, my problem isn't with you, Peaches. So calm down with all that loud shit, you tryna get shit hot. Now, my problem is with your uppity ass homegirl," she spoke while staring right at me. "Diamond, what can we possibly have in common that would make you have a problem with me?" I spoke up in my defense.

"What we got in common is Trey, bitch. If you don't play your position like the key player, one of us sitting on the benches would love to play," Diamond said sarcastically.

"Bitch please, if my man can be taken from me and that's a big "IF," then he was never mine in the first place. I don't have to make myself known to you hoes, you are a nobody. Trey does a good job of letting the world know that we are together. Now, you don't even know me but yet you feel the need to address me about MY man. I feel bad for you if you think you would ever be able to take my position. While you're a diamond in the rough, I'm a ruby bitch, we got nothing in common. Now, if you would excuse me, I did just purchase a $200.00 outfit so I can go fuck the shit out of MY man, with my upitty ass!"

I left them bitches standing there, I knew they didn't want no smoke. Sometimes you have to drop jewels on bitches and walk away.

"Damn you shut that shit down real quick," Peaches edged me on while trying to keep up with me.

"Girl bitches these days will hate you for shit you can't control, like your nigga being in love with you. I don't have time to be fighting every bitch who pussy get a little wet for fantasizing over my nigga, Trey ain't going nowhere and neither am I."

"I can't relate," She retorted.

We left the mall with no other plans, I had my share of drama for the day. We rolled another blunt before she dropped me off. I hugged Peaches goodbye and left some weed in her cup holder, I knew she probably just about smoked all hers.

Trey had already texted me, letting me know he was out handling business and would be a little late. I wasn't trippin' though, that gave me more time to get myself together.

After I got out of the shower and got into my lingerie, I set the mood for the room. That's when I heard the alarm disarm, and knew it was my baby. I heard him coming up the stairs, creeping like he usually does. I sat on the edge of the bed with my long shiny legs glistening in the dark. Trey turned on our bedroom light, as soon as his eyes locked on my body he was all over me.

"Damn Ma, you look good as hell," he said while licking his lips. "Well, I did it all for you, T. Now turn out the lights so I can light these candles and show you what a good boy you have been."

Trey turned the lights out and put in John B's cd as he undressed and laid across the bed. Grinding my hips and swaying my body to the music, I was doing my thing in

5-inch stilettos. Trey's manhood was at full attention and I didnt even touch him yet. Once the song finished I got on my hands and knees, I put all of Trey in my mouth, gagging a couple of times as his 9-inch dick hit my tonsils.

"Ummm, Baby! Damn, that shit feels so good" Trey moaned. I kept working my magic as I grabbed his balls and put them in my mouth with his dick at the same time. Trey grabbed my head and tried to stop me, but I wasn't stopping. I wanted him to feel pure ecstasy, he deserved it. Once I was done giving him the best head job I could manage, I jumped right on his hard rod and rode him like a jockey. I moaned and cried out as he penetrated in and out of me. I came already, but I continued as my white cum covered his entire manhood. After I rode his shaft like a dog in heat, Trey picked me up and fucked me on the wall. My legs were wide open, as they dangled over his arms. He lifted me into the air as my back sat against the wall. He held me in position while eating my pussy. "Oh my god, Trey," a loud sigh escaped my lips as I squirted right in his mouth. Trey's mouth was covered in my juices, so I licked it off and turned around, assuming the doggy position. Digging deep into my wet box, all I could do was bury my head into the sheets and bite my lips. My legs started trembling and I was tossing my pussy back at him rapidly, he started smacking my ass and pulling my hair, digging deeper inside of me with each thrust. "Damn, Ang! This my pussy, right?" Trey asked out of breath. "Yes, baby! This is all your pussy," I moaned with my hands rubbing against his balls. The sweet talk intensified the pleasure as he went in and out of me forcefully. "Baby, I'm about to cum," Trey bellowed as he continued to pump in and out of me. I knew he was on the verge of climaxing, I turned around and opened my mouth just in time for his warm cream to hit the back of my throat. I swallowed every drop and watched my baby collapse right next to me. My pussy was throbbing but a smile of pleasure was written across my face. A bitch must have been stupid if she thought I was given up my position. This is my man and I would ride him and ride for him till death do us part.

CHAPTER 6
TREY

---

*F*inally a nigga got his needs met. Whatever point Angela was trying to make, she sure as hell made it last night. A nigga was smiling from ear to ear. But, with pleasure comes pain. I had to get back on my grind and listen to the streets talk. Since the vicious attack on Angela, I had my young street soldiers working overtime to gather any valuable information. Word on the streets was a young nigga name Cam was hired to make a hit on Angela, when he saw she was the wife of a boss, he spared her life. I wanted to find out who was responsible for hiring the hitman, so I could lay both of them niggas out.

My man Marv got locked up on some distribution charges and the Feds picked that shit up real quick. I had to stay out the way for a minute, I felt like I couldn't trust anyone. For some reason Marvin has been acting shady, something was telling me to put heat on his ass. Niggas fold under pressure, but since it was my weight he got caught with I wasn't trying to get caught up in no shit. Marv got locked up four days ago and was out the same day. Man, I know for a fact that nigga had to be turning snitch. Ain't no way in hell you get a Fed case and don't post bail, but you out on an ankle monitor. Now, all of a sudden he blowing my phone up, but when I was trying to get at the nigga after I got out of the hospital, he was nowhere to be found. Niggas kept telling me my right-hand man was low key jealous of me, I didn't want to believe that shit though. Marv and I grew up from the sandbox, baggin' and smashing bitches together, I got the opportunity to make serious bread and Marv was the first nigga I put on.

I snapped out of my thoughts and continued to drive. As I was cruising down Lexington and Broadway, one of my street soldiers named Crazy Carl waved me over. Putting my truck in park, I hopped out and we gave each other a pound.

"Yo! What's up Boss Man. I hear these streets have been talkin' recklessly about your boy Marvin. Word is, he hired Cam to take out Angela on some jealous shit," Carl explained.

"Man, why would Marv want to take Angela out, she wasn't hard in this shit?" I questioned. I had to hold my composure, I knew damn well Marv couldn't have been this bitch made. "Listen Boss Man," Carl rubbed his head and then continued. "You were down for a little over a month, Angela was holding shit down like a boss wifey supposed to. One day Marv got in his feelings and crossed the line. I heard she bust that nigga in his mouth and left him standing there. I guess he was embarrassed and wanted her out of the way."

I could feel my muscles tighten in my neck, my trigger finger was ready. I continued to listen to Carl, hoping to get more info.

"The thing is this boss, Marvin never told Cam who he wanted dead, he gave him 10 stacks to kill. Cam was pressed for a quick come up, so of course, he took the job. That is until he saw who she was and spared her life." I stood there in a rage not knowing what to say, my baby was out here putting niggas in their place. I gathered my thoughts before speaking. "Listen, Carl, I want that nigga Marv gone. I need to see Cam face to face, so I can hear this shit out that nigga mouth before I take his life. I respect that he didn't kill Angela, but what I don't respect is him kicking my unborn seed out of her." Carl's mouth dropped, it was obvious that the streets didn't tell that part. "Damn I'm sorry, Boss," was all he could muster up. "It's all good Carl. Thanks for the 411, just keep a lookout on them niggas. They got a bounty on their heads."

I jumped back in my truck and popped in my Tupac CD: "2 Of Amerikaz Most Wanted," thumping out my speakers had me ready for war. I couldn't move any weight because I felt like the Feds were watching me.

Every turn I made it felt like I was being followed, I would stay low until further notice. While I was staying low I would plot on how to take these two niggas out. Somebody had already tipped me off with Cam's address out in Philly. I already knew where Marv was. It was just a matter of time before I caught up with him. As I was cruising the streets my mind wouldn't let me shake what was done to Angela. So, I texted her and told her I love her and that I'd be home later than expected. Making sure I had my bitch loaded and ready to bust, I headed out to Philly. Cam would have an unexpected visitor today.

As I exited the interstate, my GPS was showing that I was only 2 minutes away from Cam's spot. I would lay low out of sight and scope the place out before making any moves.

It was almost 11 o'clock. I've been sitting out here for about 2 hours, seeing some people go in and out. For the last hour, there was no traffic and Cam was still inside. I got my bitch(pistol) in place and made moves down the street. I wore dark colors, an all-black hoodie, black sweatpants, and black Timbs. If I was anywhere else I'd probably look suspicious, but on the streets of Philly, I looked like an average nigga. I made my way to the back of the house, checking the door first; it was locked. I went to the window and that shit was unlocked. "BINGO!"

I entered the house hearing the sound of a TV. It also sounded like a bitch screaming while getting her pussy banged out. I slowly checked my surroundings before creeping upstairs, I followed the noise. I poked my head into the second room on the right, my fingers started itching at the sight before me. Cam was pounding some bitch out, they were so into it they didn't hear me. I made my way behind him. I caught him with his pants down, literally.

"Get yo bitch ass up nigga," I ordered him off the bed. When he got up my blood started boiling as I saw it was Peaches he was fucking. "Peaches turn ya ass around unless you want this heat too," I advised her. "So, Cam. I heard you paid a visit to my home unannounced and put hands on my queen," I questioned him while shoving my pistol in his stomach. "Man, I didn't know that was your wifey. When I saw it was her I took flight," Cam said while stuttering. "You took flight after you kicked her in her stomach, making her lose my unborn child you bitch ass nigga." I pistol-whipped him, hitting him a few times in his face.

"Now, be a real man and tell me how this shit went down, and why?" It didn't take Cam long to start singing like a bird. "Well, Marv asked me to take a hit, so I did. He was paying 10 stacks and I was fucked up, I didn't know where the hit was, so Marv told me to get up with Peaches and she would let me know which house to hit."

I looked at Peaches in disgust. "You sold your homegirl out, you dirty ass trick bitch," I said furiously. Peaches just balled up and cried. "You know what Cam," I was standing in front of him, looking him right in his fucked up eye. "You are a loyal ass soldier and I wish you were on my team, at some point. However, under these circumstances I can't walk the same streets as you, you fucked up when you touched what belonged to me." I cocked my pistol back and unloaded the clip as he went limp. I ended his life by putting four bullets in him; two to his head and two to his heart. Before walking out I grabbed Peaches by her hair and pistol-whipped her ass. "If you ever try to come near Angela, I'll kill your grimey ass. You lucky I don't lay your ass out right next to that snake."

I left the house, disappearing in the night and never looking back. I jumped back in my whip, bumping Tupac "Me and My Girlfriend."

CHAPTER 7

ANGELA

For the past week, Trey has been acting funny. If there's a knock at the door he panics, if I'm gone too long he panics; he's never stayed home as much as he has, but I'm not complaining.

For some reason, Peaches was ignoring my calls. I was just going to pop up at her house, but I just left it alone. If a bitch wanted to be all in these niggas faces, rather than kicking it with her homegirl, so be it.

Since I had nothing else to do, I thought I'd just cater to my man. I had to ease Trey's mind. Something was bothering him, and it was written all over his face. I went into the kitchen to take out food to prepare dinner. I had to feed Trey first, then, suck the shit out of him. Maybe then he would loosen up a little. Even though we ate out a lot at the most expensive restaurants, I made sure we had food at home as well. I was making steak, loaded potatoes, oven-roasted asparagus, and dressing. One thing I knew how to do was cook, I made sure Trey always came home to a meal. After I prepared dinner I sat everything on the table and called Trey in from his man cave. Whenever he was cooped up in his cave, I knew something had to be heavy on his brain. "Damn Ma, you got it smelling like a 5-star restaurant in here," Trey said as he grabbed me around my waist and kissed me. "All for you, daddy" I replied while kissing him passionately. We sat down and enjoyed most of our meal in silence.

Breaking the silence, I asked Trey what was wrong.

"Listen, Ang." Trey began to talk as he held my hand. He looked straight into my eyes, and I could tell something was seriously wrong. "Your boy got into some serious shit." My heart dropped. I didn't know what was going on, Trey usually kept me out of his street business. "Whatever it is, I'm sure we can get through it. As long as you ain't cheating on me or expecting a baby we good." I chuckled a little, trying to lighten the mood."

"Nah, it ain't nothing like that beautiful. You know you my one and only queen and I'd never disrespect you like that," Trey said seriously. I was so deeply in love with my man, I stood up and walked over to Trey dropping down to my knees. I was on my period heavy, I couldn't fuck him, but I sure could give him some bomb ass head.

"Damn Ang! what you bout to do to a nigga?" Trey asked while shifting in his chair, looking pleased. I just ignored him and took his long shaft out and put it in my mouth, my saliva covering his wood and dripping down to his balls. I started making a gurgling sound because I knew that drove him crazy. All I could hear was Trey's moans, and that shit was turning me on so I started going super head crazy, slurping, gagging, swallowing. I was going wild, doing the most. After I calmed down I took his balls and dick in my mouth at the same time, I called that the three-piece. I was careful, if you didn't master this right it could be uncomfortable and ruin the whole mood. I was easy with him until I took the balls out, I played with them while jerking him. Trey had my hair pulling it and biting down on his lips. I loved when he did that shit he looked so sexy. I began jerking his dick fast while sucking his balls lightly. "I'm about to cum, baby." He managed to get out between stutters. That was my cue to go hard, I tightened my jaw bone around his stiff wood. As I was getting back into the rhythm, Trey's legs started to shake letting me know he was on the verge of climaxing. My rhythm was interrupted when our door was kicked off its hinges.

"Freeze!"

"Put your fucking hands in the air. Get down now!"

I was in a state of shock and didn't know what the hell was going on. I turned and looked at Trey as he stood up with his dick hanging and his hands in the air. About fifteen cops swarmed past me and tussled with Trey, slamming him on the floor. The sly smile on his face aggravated them even more, so they kicked him repeatedly.

"Stop fucking kicking him before you hurt him," I yelled while trying to make my way over to him.

"Ma'am, listen, if you don't stand back, you'll be in cuffs right along with him," a rookie officer was the only one who spoke up. Everyone else walked around collecting shit, I knew they wouldn't find anything here. Whatever was going on, I knew Trey was smart.

"What the fuck is going on," I asked the officer who was closer to me. "I think it would have been a lot better if you would have knocked instead of tearing down my damn door," I damn near shouted in his ear. "Well, unfortunately, we have the right to do what the hell we want to do," a fat officer with a size too small uniform said.

"Trey Issac Godfrey you are under arrest for the murder of Cameron Ellington." The officer started reading Trey his rights; while the other officer handcuffed him. I was lost, I didn't know who Trey would want to murder. I played it cool as any real woman should. "Listen, Baby, don't worry. I'll have your attorney on it as soon as possible. We all know you're innocent and they're just trying to pin anything on you," I said as they escorted my love out the house into a waiting police car. As I walked to the door I was in dismay; it looked like the entire police academy was outside our house. My baby was into some shit and I didn't know what the hell was going on, but a murder charge was not what I was expecting. Instead of crying like I wanted to, I jumped right on the phone with Trey's attorney and let him know what was going on. He said he would get right on top of it but would need $50,000 upfront with the kind of charges Trey was facing. After hanging up from Trey's attorney I called Peaches, again I was sent straight to voicemail. I needed her at this moment but I guess I had to handle business by myself. I hopped in the shower and put on an Adidas jogging suit. I tied my hair pack in a ponytail. This isn't my normal attire, but I was dressed for the occasion.

My first stop was to the bank, I had to get some cash to pay the attorney. After I withdrew the money, I sat in the parking lot to call the courts. I needed to find out as much information as I could before my meeting. After leaving the bank I stopped to grab a soda and headed to Carlton and Rivers Law Firm to hear what Rivers had to say about Trey's case.

"Hello, Angela," Rivers greeted me. I stood up and shook his hand as he led me to his office. "Okay Angela," Rivers began.

"I've been looking into this case all morning since you called me, Trey is being held without bail as it is expected when someone is accused of murder. He was positively identified by an eyewitness to the murder, and the prosecuting DA is holding her in a witness protection program."

"It's a chick?" I asked, cutting him off for the first time.

"Yes, according to the DA it's a female who knows Trey personally and she was there when the murder took place," Rivers said. My mind was racing full speed and I felt dizzy as if at any moment I'd pass out. "Angela are you ok? Would you like a cup of water?" Rivers asked, looking very concerned. "No, I'm ok, I'm just trying to register all this."

"Well, how can we get Trey out of this?" I wanted an answer, but I also knew there was no way out of this shit.

"Well, to be honest, it's going to take a lot of time and convincing. Usually, when there is a witness they already feel like they've won."

"If there is no witness then there is no case, right?" I said as a statement rather than a question. "You're right

Angela. But if you don't know who the witness is, then you have no chance of persuading them not to take that stand," Rivers said, looking at me knowingly. "Well, Rivers thanks for your time." I gave him the money and headed out of his office. The first thing I'd do is hit the streets; the streets always talk and I was going to find out what they were chatting about. A bitch was a witness to a crime my man committed and she knew Trey; this shit was bothering me. What bitch in her right mind would snitch on him? My thoughts were all over the place, I had to figure out my next move. Even if the bitch was in a witness protection program she could still be touched, I was about to get heavy in this shit and I didn't even know it.

CHAPTER 8
TREY

---

*E*ven though I knew this day would come back to haunt me, I wasn't prepared for it. That shit fucked me up when the cops said I was being arrested for murder. I was laying low thinking this nigga Marv was trying to set me up on some drug charges, that was the least of my worries. My dumb ass let a witness live. Sitting in the jail cell had a nigga deep in thought. I knew the rules of the streets and I didn't obey rule number two; leave no witnesses. Rule number one; never shit where you eat. I followed that rule no matter what. If I didn't, Angela would have gone down too. That's why I keep stash spots all over the damn city. I fucked up big time, since I beat the bitch up, I knew she wouldn't mind ratting me out. It wasn't too much I could do, being behind bars. I had to get word to my street soldiers about this shit, hopefully, they could find this bitch whereabouts.

I was still waiting to be classified, knowing this shit could take forever. I just tried to stay calm and keep my mind off my mistakes that got me here. The last time I got locked up, Angela was out there in the streets heavy. I wasn't trying to have her out there like that again. When my baby told me she lost our seed and a nigga touched her, something inside of me broke. I didn't show it to Angela, but I was hurt like crazy. I still had to see that nigga Marv and lay him to rest, his time was up.

I knew Angela would be here soon as I'm allowed visits, so I had to let her know the truth as to why I'm here in the first place. I wasn't expecting to get caught up this damn fast, so I didn't have time to tell her what was going on. Then again, I should probably wait to tell her. My mind was everywhere. I didn't know If I was coming or going. I didn't want Angela stressing either, so I was just going to tell her they tryna pin a body on me.

Finally, a CO came to the cell and opened it, he told the other nigga to come out to get classified.

"Yo man I was here 4 hours before this dude," I told the CO

"Boy sit your black ass down, You're not going anywhere anytime soon with a murder charge dude," the CO shot back. I wanted to knock the fucking smirk off that pig's face, but what good would that do but make my situation worse than what it was. I sat back down on the cold metal bench trying to keep calm as possible. Time was of the essence, and I didnt have it to waste.

My mind wouldn't let me stop thinking about Peaches' grimey ass and how she turned on Angela. That's another reason I should've deaded that bird bitch. I couldn't keep beating myself up though. I was a chess player and I had to make my next move my best move. See what I've come to learn is that, once people feel you've hit rock bottom and they have one up on you, they start getting sloppy. Eventually, they'll leave a trail leading right to their asses, and once that happens CHECKMATE…

CHAPTER 9
ANGELA

Two months later:

*K*nowing Trey was back in that hell hole just breaks my heart into a million and one-pieces, I hated this shit. He didn't show it, but I knew it was killing him being in there. They had my baby housed in Rikers Island, which was only one hour from home, but I hated what I heard about that prison. Trey's Mom usually rode with me to visit him, since Trey didn't like me driving alone. This particular day I went alone, I rode the bus so we could have a private visit. I wasn't going to let Trey know I knew more than what he was telling me. The lawyer already gave me a tip by telling me a bitch witnessed him murdering someone. But, Trey said they were just trying to pin a body on him. I knew that was a lie, and I was going to find out. One thing I always did was keep my ears open, I was a nosy bitch. I wanted to know what Trey was hiding from me, I didn't want to ask him over the phone, or on the visit. I had no other choice but to wait.

Not Knowing who the bitch was who held the key to Trey's future was one of my biggest problems. I was the only bitch who needed the key to his future and his heart.

The visiting room door opened and Trey came out looking sexy as ever, he always made a bad situation look so damn good. He was rocking his new black and white Nikes I sent him, a button-up white Polo shirt, green state pants, and he had a fresh cut and trim. His walk was his trademark, just by the way he walked, you could tell it was him from a mile away; with his sexy ass. Once he approached the table, he grabbed my ass and hugged me tightly. I loved seeing my man, but I wanted him home. The visit was going smoothly until Trey started getting serious towards the end.

"Listen Ma, I'll be out of here soon. I got my street soldiers working on shit for me," Trey said with confidence. "Well, if this is supposed to be a bogus charge like you claim, why do you need your street soldiers to take care of anything when you have a lawyer?" Trey realized he slipped up. He looked at me seriously before trying to grab my hands. The CO looked over at us suspiciously, so he let go and finished talking. "Ang, I never lie to you, but I'm in some deep shit and I rather you not know at this point. I'm only trying to protect you and the only way for me to do that behind these walls is not telling you some things." I tried holding in my tears because I didn't want to seem weak.

Trey told me everything would be alright and I believed him. I also knew something was up. I needed to do my homework to find out what was going on, and why Trey was being accused of murder as soon as I was back in the city. Trey and I sat there and discussed how things were going with me; he stressed the issue about me staying out the way and letting his men handle his business. I didn't blame him for feeling that way, the incident that happened last time broke him. We kissed each other goodbye and hugged one last time before the CO instructed everyone to leave.

Leaving to go back home without my man was always the worst part. The ride home seemed like forever, I sat in my seat thinking about my girl Peaches and wondered why she just dipped out on me like I was a bird bitch. One day we were laughing, shopping, and chilling, and then she stopped answering my calls, and that led to her cutting her phone off or changing her number. Peaches was my best friend, the only friend I had. With her sudden disappearance, I was getting really worried about her. Then the situation with Marvin hit me. Maybe he told Peaches I hit him and made it seem like I was trying to get at him or something. Damn. I never thought about that. Even if he did tell her about that incident, I would still expect Peaches to call me and ask me what happened. Then again, Peaches was always about these niggas. If a nigga blew her a kiss, her pussy would cum. That's just how she has always been. My only choice was to get more information from the streets. I would pay a visit to Peaches neighborhood and see what I could find out. As the bus made its way towards the city it passed through New Jersey to drop some folks off. I was just looking around and low and behold Peaches was walking. I know I wasn't hallucinating, I knew my girl from a mile away just by the way she dressed. I wanted to hop off the bus and check her, but before I could get to the front the bus was pulling off. Now, what the hell was she doing way down here in Jersey? I knew Peaches damn near all my life and she was a city girl; she stuck out like a sore thumb walking Jersey streets. Something just didn't seem right and I had to find out what the hell was up with her.

Finally, I got home. I hopped in the shower, then threw on a sweatsuit, and jumped in the Mercedes. I didn't feel like driving the Escalade today. I was headed up to Peaches' old neighborhood in Queens.

Once I arrived, I walked up to Peaches' door, hoping I wouldn't see Marvin's sorry ass. I knocked over and over again, but no answer. Of course, everyone outside the projects was always lit. A young boy saw me knocking and made his way over to where I was. I reached in my purse and gripped my .22 just in case a nigga wanted to get froggy.

"Yo Ma, If you are looking for Marv, you ain't gonna find him there. But, If you looking for some work I got you," the boy said. "Nah. I'm actually looking for Peaches," I told him. He smirked and started laughing like something was funny.

"Listen, lady," you and everybody else looking for Peaches. If you think that bitch just gone open the door and welcome you with open arms you crazy ass hell. You need to take your pretty ass back to Manhattan because from the looks of it you ain't from 'round here."

"Well, why would anyone be looking for Peaches? Is she in trouble?" I wanted to seem like I was extremely concerned. "I'm her sister, I just got into town today and this is the last address she gave me."

"I hate to be the bearer of bad news, but your sister got a bounty on her head."

"What do you mean by that?" "Well, if I'm giving up any more information, you're going to have to pay for my services," he challenged with that same ugly smirk on his face. I peeled off two- hundred and handed it to him and he told me everything he knew. "Peaches got caught up in some shit, she witnessed a murder and turned snitch, now she's running for her life. The bounty on her head is $100,000 so you know all of NYC looking for her. She was in a witness protection program, but when a crooked cop tried to take her life she ended up bouncing on their asses too. The man she was supposed to snitch on is a known drug lord, who ended up bodying a nigga and pistol-whipping Peaches. That was the wrong move, sparing her life got the nigga behind bars. Peaches don't sit in one spot for too long, so good luck finding her. I'm Stylez by the way."

He filled me in on all the pieces I was missing from the puzzle. I handed him another $100 and jumped back in my car and took off. Now, everything was making more sense, but I still didn't understand why Peaches and Trey were together. I was still kind of lost but that explained why she stopped answering my calls and cut me off completely. She was the reason my man was locked the fuck up. Peaches hood ass was a fucking rat. I was going to find this bitch, and when I did, shit was about to get ugly. I had the perfect plan. Peaches would run from anything besides a nigga, and since Stylez provided me with all that information he was about to become apart of my game. I was about to put my plans in motion and nothing would stop me from executing the death sentence this bitch deserved. Since she wanted to be a rat, I would be the snake and watch the life drain out of her. I headed back home smiling inside knowing that my ex-best friend's fate laid in my hands. If anyone would be collecting that $100,000 bounty, it would be me.

CHAPTER 10
PEACHES

$\mathcal{M}$y life turned from bad to worse, I never been on the run all of my 25 years of life. I did a lot of dirty shit, but this time was by far the dirtiest thing I've done. I turned on my best friend, causing her to lose her unborn child, and then snitching on her man. All that only got me to where I'm at now, RUNNING.

Even though I'm no punk bitch, Trey is so fucking notorious he can send a hit from behind them damn bars. I think he already did, why else would a cop try to kill me. He had to be on Trey's payroll. I've known Trey forever, so it's sad to say I took his street credibility for a joke and that was my first mistake. I was paying for it tremendously now.

I decided to leave my hotel room and get some air. I've been cooped up in there for two weeks now. I was saving all my money they were giving me in the witness protection program, I'm glad I did or I wouldn't have a pot to piss in. Putting on my headphones, I made my way up Lincoln Street past a bus terminal. I didn't have a destination and I didnt know where the hell I was going, I just wanted to walk since nobody knew me here in Jersey. As I was approaching the bus terminal people started getting off the bus. So, I kept it moving; bobbing my head like I didn't have a care in the world. As I got closer to the bus my heart dropped, to my surprise, Angela was sitting on the bus. I wanted to hug her so badly, but knowing the way she loved Trey, she would probably kill me right there. I just kept walking hoping she didn't see me. I put my head down and kept bouncing to the beat. Seeing Angela on that bus fucked my head up. I guess I wasn't the only one that was doing bad. Angela's prissy ass would never be seen riding a bus, Trey's absence must have taken its toll on her for her to be riding public transportation. As much as I felt bad for her, Trey still got what he deserved. That nigga broke my damn nose and I had to have reconstructive surgery on my face. My heart ached for Angela, but my heart pumped hate for Trey. I'm pretty sure Angela didn't recognize me so I carried on about my day; walking the streets getting familiar with my new hometown. Nobody would think I'd be residing in Jersey. I began to get acquainted with people and hang out more, hoping that would help me stop being so paranoid. My ass was on the run from everybody, so I had to make sure I switched up my looks all the time. The FBI still wanted me to testify against Trey, so they were on my ass too. I was the key witness; matter of fact the only witness. But there was no way I could go through with this shit.

After a while, I began to get careless by partying and getting high. I met a chick who was cool as fuck, and she kept me hip to Jersey. Every night we were in somebody's club or some niggas whip; smoking up all their shit and drinking until we were overly satisfied. My life started looking a lot better. I was even able to sleep at night without having nightmares of being killed. Life was turning around for me up to the point I met a young dude from the city who just relocated to Jersey. He told me his name was Justice, but for some reason, he hesitated when I asked. He always wore the latest gear, looking fresh and well-kept. His neat cornrows meshed well with his neatly trimmed mustache. He was so damn sexy; he made my pussy wet every time I was in his presence. I met him while partying at a club and he just stood out. The only thing that was awkward about him was that ugly ass smirk he kept on his face. I stopped partying with the chick I met and my focus was all on him. Everybody who knew me knew that these niggas were my weakness. He was either heaven-sent or the gift from the devil, either way, I was feeling him. The crazy thing is he just seemed to pop up from nowhere. But, I like a mystery guy and hopefully, he liked this freaky girl.

I wasn't on my Ps and Qs anymore. I felt like Justice would protect me if some shit popped off, that's how much he was feeling me. I began to get careless; forgetting that I still had a bounty on my head. But I didn't even give a fuck anymore. I had a nigga who was all about me, I felt like I couldn't be touched. The only person that would ever get close to touching me was him, if I knew how true that statement was I swear I'd take it back

CHAPTER 11
TREY

---

8 MONTHS LATER:

*L*ifting weights in the yard was starting to become a habit for me, I had to put my mind on something else besides spending the rest of my life behind bars at Rikers Island. Angela was always on the wifey duties and making sure I was good with money and fresh gear. My baby always made sure there was money on the phone, she came to see me twice a month. I've been locked down for a year now and these faggots kept postponing my damn court dates, talking about they can't locate the witness. My patience was wearing thin, I was hoping with the bounty I put on Peaches head she was somewhere slumped.

Then, to make matters worse I've been hearing this nigga Marvin done got his weight up. He fled the city and started moving weight in Philly. That shit blew my damn mind. He went from my right-hand man and partner in crime to a fucking rat. The whole time I've been on lockdown I haven't heard from him. Shit crazy, the same mufuckaz you put on be the same ones to shit on you. I tried not to stress the street life, most of my niggas done shited on me like I was already sentenced to life and wouldn't be back in them streets.

"Yo, Trey, You good? You look like you ready to kill somebody," a nigga name Frank said as he snapped me out of my thought. "Yeah. I'm good, big homie," I assured him. I put the weights down and dropped down and started doing push-ups. See the thing about me is, I got respect everywhere I went. I ain't have no problems in prison, most of these niggas were dick riders and I ain't gay. I hated for a nigga to be on my dick. When you get the money, you get power and respect, I was used to this shit. My life in another human being's hand was not something I was used to. That shit right there had a nigga going crazy.

Once the C.O.s started coming I knew it was time to go back to our cells. I gathered my shit up and made my way towards the gate, some lame-ass nigga bumped into me causing me to lose my balance. I turned around staring him right in his eyes, and he had the nerve to twist his face up at me.

"Yo, my bad, Trey." He let out a sinister chuckle.

"Nigga, do I know you?"

"Naw. You don't know me, but I know you, my nigga Marv said you pussy."

Before I knew it, I two-pieced him and blood flew from his mouth. All the New York niggas made their way over by me, we all handed that nigga an ass-whooping.

COs came from all over the prison hitting everybody with clubs, niggas was dropping like flies. Before I could drop to my knees I was hit hard as fuck in my stomach and on my back; I got the wind knocked out of me and fell to the ground in unbearable pain. About twenty of us were chained up and thrown in double lock for 60 days. I still didnt know who the nigga was who tried to press me on Marv's behalf. But that nigga probably wouldn't talk again, his jaw was super twisted and he probably swallowed about a good four teeth. I didn't need help fighting him though, but when you behind these walls it's a respect thing.

Angela came up to see me and was pissed she had to talk to me through a glass window. A no-contact visit is what the shit was since I was in double lockdown. Seeing her just brightened up my day; her beautiful smile, thick thighs, and full breast had my dick on swole. Being locked down for a year had me wanting to break the window that separated Ang and me. I wanted to climb right into her wet and warm pussy.

"Trey! Trey!"

I snapped out of my trance as I heard Angela calling my name. "Damn boy, what the fuck you over there fantasizing about?" Angela asked with a look of confusion on her face. "My bad Ang, but you look real good and I couldn't help but think about pounding that pussy out," I replied trying to ease the tension.

Lately, Angela has been acting a little off and I didnt know why. I was wondering if the streets were talking and she heard some shit. Not being able to kiss her or touch her only made the situation worse. So, for the remainder of the visit, I just poured out my heart to her. With me being locked up I knew she had to be going through a lot out there. I let her know how much I appreciated her. As the visit was coming to an end, Angela looked at me with a look of concern. "I hope you aren't holding any secrets, when bitches bodies start dropping I don't want any regrets." Staring into Angela's eyes, I was speechless. I didn't know what she meant by that, I was hoping she wasn't being fed lies out there. All I could do was mouth "I love you," before she put the phone down and exited the visiting room.

After the visit, I couldn't help but wonder what Angela was referring to. I tried to let it go, but for some reason, her words kept playing over and over in my head. I had to hurry up and get out of here. I couldn't let these streets devour my queen. Angela was on some other shit and I had to make sure she was good. The way she is talking be having me on the edge. I didn't know what Angela knew or what people were telling her. But what I did know was somebody better collect that bounty on that bitch Peaches head fast, I needed to get out of here and back to my wifey. Angela was my queen and I was going to show her that when I got out of here. I wanted to marry her and plant my seeds in her. It was just a matter of time before these gates would open and I'd be free, but the thing is, I just didn't know when or how long.

CHAPTER 12
ANGELA

---

*B*eing away from Trey for so long had me ready to break down, but I knew I had to be strong. On our last visit, I was a little hard on him; but I was also pissed. Not only did he get into a fight, but we also had to communicate through a big piece of fucking glass. I was also having mixed emotions about the situation with him and Peaches, why were they together in the first place, and why he never told me is what bothered me. Even though I was mad at Trey, I needed him home with me. I was already getting everything into motion; it was just a matter of time before I could execute my plan. With Stylez on my payroll, I just knew everything would go as planned. I eventually told him Peaches and I were not sisters and that I was the wife of the boss she was responsible for putting behind bars. At first, he was a little skeptical, but when I laid out 6 digit figures to him he couldn't resist my offer. Stylez was more afraid of being in my presence, knowing how ruthless Trey was. I assured him as long as he did not cross me, he had nothing to worry about. After the long day I had, I needed some wine and a bath.

I was still running the empire as usual and I was just tired. Making drops and making sure the street soldiers were all on point, had me drained. It was time to give my pussy the attention it deserved. I made my way upstairs and ran some bath water, lit some candles, and put my wine on the side of the tub. I had to go back into my room and grab my vibrating bullet; I call it "Boom!" Making my way back into the bathroom, I got into the tub and it felt like my body was melting right in the water. I guzzled my wine and felt my juicy pussy as it began to pulsate with every touch. Moans escaped my mouth as I inserted Boom in and out of my throbbing pussy. I was in pure bliss and managed to get one orgasm off in a matter of seconds. My chest heaved up and down as I tried to catch my breath. I was ready to climax and my legs started shaking, splashing water everywhere. Finally, I released all the tension built up inside of me. I laid back with a sinister smile on my face, as my evil plan crossed my mind and revenge was so close I could taste it.

I got out of the tub feeling refreshed, my mind was focused, and my needs were met. Before I could get dressed my phone went off with several notifications; letting me know I just received a few text messages. I made my way over to my phone and smiled when I saw the messages were from Stylez. One text was a picture of Peaches sitting at the bar, and another picture of the both of them taking a selfie. Under the picture, he sent a message that said,

"My loyalty will remain with you. Believe that." I knew Stylez was trying to gain my trust, and so far he was doing a good job of winning me over. All I needed now was a plan that wouldn't tie either me or him into this twisted plot I was about to create. Sometimes the perfect plan is not so perfect and I didnt want to make any mistakes that would cost us our freedom. Styles tried to take his time with Peached, he didn't want her to think he was rushing anything and make himself look suspicious.

The first time they met was at a bar and she fell right for him, but another nigga who wasn't apart of our plan ended up getting Peaches' attention and she stopped answering Stylez's calls. Finally, after another two months of trying to locate and track her down, Stylez ran back into her at Envy Nightclub, that's where he took the pictures he sent to me. I was a little hard on him; telling him every other day he better find that bitch. Slowly but surely he did. Excitement warmed my body. All I wanted was Peaches' body to be floating somewhere in the river by now. But I knew making moves too quick would only fuck up the plan.

Texting Stylez back, I replied, **"Loyalty over everything, Meet me at the spot in 20 minutes."**
I got dressed, wearing a black and red jogging suit, all red Jordans, and a black and red Chicago Bulls jacket. Walking out of my house, I was on a mission. With Peaches' dick happy ass back in the picture, I felt more confident that Trey would be out of jail soon. Jumping into the whip, I made my way down Main street to meet Stylez at a secluded Chinese spot off of Delaware, I didn't need everyone in my business, and I didn't want people seeing me with Stylez. For one, rumors get spread too fast. Secondly, I wanted to make sure if we were to ever get questioned, no one would know we were even connected in any way. I made my way into the spot and Stylez was already seated. As I approached the table, he stood up and hugged me, he remained standing until I sat down. Whoever raised him taught him some manners. I could see a lot of Trey in Stylez, that's why I brought him on board. "So, Mrs. Boss Lady, what's up?" Stylez began the conversation. "Well, I just wanted to touch bases with you to make sure your head is still in this and you haven't fallen in love," I replied. Stylez chuckled before saying, "Listen here, Boss Lady, I think with my head at all times; I calculate my steps and I make sure I'm always two steps ahead. If I couldn't handle this job, I wouldn't have taken you up on your offer."

"Furthermore, Peaches just ain't my type. A female who can hop dick to dick just ain't for me."

"Ok. Ok." I cut him off before he could continue. "To be honest, Stylez, the reason I even brought you aboard, is that I see a lot of my man in you. You're a younger version of Trey, I can tell a loyal soldier by how he presents himself. I've known you a little over a year and you have proven yourself more than some of the cats that have been on Trey's payroll for over 5 years."

Stylez nodded his head in approval. "Ok, now let's cut the small talk and get to the big things," I said in a playful tone. Stylez pulled out a notepad. On the pad was a diagram with Peaches' name in big bold letters. Looking at the details on that paper I could tell things were going to get interesting, I just sat back, folded my arms, and let Stylez talk about his plan. One thing I had to tell him was, I was going to be a part of this plan, so he needed to add me in there somewhere. Stylez wanted to execute the plan alone, he thought I should stay low and make sure Trey was good.

Before getting up and leaving the table, I looked back at Stylez and said, "If anyone will be pulling that trigger, it will be me."

CHAPTER 13
PEACHES

S itting on the bed in the hotel room smoking a blunt, I blew smoke in pure bliss. Justice just put it on me real good and a bitch was feeling herself. He seemed to be taking longer than usual, so I made my way towards the bathroom. I noticed the water was no longer running. "Everything is taken care of, Sis. You have nothing to worry about, Meet me at the spot in an hour," I heard him say before hanging up the phone.

After eavesdropping I made my way back towards the bed. Before I sat down he came out of the bathroom wrapped in a towel. "So you got a sister you haven't told me about," I asked. Justice looked at me agitated before responding, "Yeah, I got a little sister who just got into town. She wants to kick it for a short, so I'm going to meet her at the bar off Norfolk."

"Well, why don't you just invite her here. I'll order some food. I'd love to meet your sister." Justice looked a little uneasy like he was in deep thought. "You know what, that doesn't sound like a bad idea, I think my sister would love to meet you too," he said. "Sounds good! Let me go hop in the shower and freshen up." I went to my suitcase where I had my clothes and decided on a white halter top with matching capris. I wanted to look decent because the first impression is everything. Making my way into the bathroom, I turned the shower on, before getting in I heard Justice back on the phone. "Change of plans, meet me at Days Inn off New Road." I smiled ear to ear knowing I was going to meet someone in his family. They say when a nigga starts introducing you to the family, then he got love for you. Call me crazy, but, I was going to make it so he wouldn't ever want to leave me. After winning his sister over, I'd be meeting his Mom and Pops too.

After showering I made sure to put on extra lotion and perfume, I slicked my hair back into a ponytail and added light makeup.

Justice and I decided on Chinese food. I ordered from down the street so delivery wouldn't take too long.

A light knock tapped the door about fifteen minutes later, I jumped up anxiously knowing that it was either the food or his sister. "It's my sister, I'll get it," Justice said, trying to beat me to the door. "No, I got it," I told him as I blew him a kiss and turned the knob at the same time.

"What are you looking at him for, aren't you going to invite me in?" An all too familiar voice whispered. I turned around quickly, to my surprise Angela was standing at the door with the food in her hand. I wanted to scream but my throat was so dry, I couldn't swallow. All of my blood felt like it drained from my face, I felt like I was staring at a ghost.

"Peaches, I'd like you to meet my sister, Angela," Justice said in a sinister voice. "That ain't your fucking sister! You set me up?" I yelled. My first instincts were to run. I tried to slam the door in Angela's face, but she overpowered me and made her way in. Justice grabbed me by my hair and slammed me on a chair.

"Damn! That ain't no way to treat family. Aren't you happy to see me? Stylez has told me so much about you," Angela said sarcastically.

"Who the fuck is Stylez?" I was confused. "Damn, you fucking a nigga and don't even know his name? Yeah, you're still the same trick ass bitch I met all of them years ago," Angela was now belittling me.

Before I could say anything my mouth was stuffed with a sock. Angela began to unload a duffle bag, The contents of the bag made me vomit in my mouth. Angela dumped gloves, a rope, lye, and so much more. Picking

65

up two knives Angela taunted me. Before I knew it, I pissed myself.

"Before I do your ass filthy, I'll allow you to talk," Angela said as she took the tape off my mouth. "Listen, Angela, I'm so sorry. Trey fucked me up when he killed Cam. But listen, I never meant for any harm to come on you. If I knew you were pregnant, I would have never dropped the dime on you. Furthermore, I would have told you Marv had $10,000 on your head." Angela looked at me puzzled. "What the fuck are you talking about? Bitch, you mean to tell me all this time it was you? My fucking baby is gone because of your trifling ass." You could see spit flying as Angela yelled. I was digging my own fucking grave. All this time I thought that was the reason this bitch was coming for me, but she didn't even know what I did. I sat with my hands taped to the chair knowing that I wouldn't make it out of this room alive. After what I just told her, I knew she wouldn't spare my life. Angela paced the room as Justice, Stylez, or whoever he was laughed at the torture I endured.

Before I knew it I had a rope around my neck. My hands were taped, so it was nothing I could do, Angela snapped, and I knew she would inflict the most excruciating pain on me that she could muster. I was going in and out of consciousness, trying to gasp for air as the rope around my neck became tighter as Stylez yanked and pulled it at Angela's request. There was no need to fight or try to say anything else, Everything I have ever done was now catching up to my ass. I knew there was no chance of me surviving the night. So, I just sat there waiting for them to put me out of my misery.

CHAPTER 14
ANGELA

*E*motions took over me, I was on an emotional rollercoaster and I couldn't get off. All this time I was thinking Peaches was just a snitch, but she was also a low-life traitor. This bitch was the reason my baby was gone. I couldn't even think straight after she said that shit. So, now it all makes sense. Trey murdered Cam and fucked this bitch up after learning she had a hand in my attack. Even after hearing her say all that out of her mouth, I wanted to let her go. Seeing her slumped like that did something to me. I sat debating a little bit longer until Stylez snapped me out of my thoughts.

"You alright, Boss Lady?" he asked in a concerned tone. "Yeah, I'm good, but I don't think we should go with our original plan though," I told him. "What you mean?" He asked, a little puzzled. "I was thinking we should keep shit clean and leave out the torturing part." Stylez nodded his head in approval. Taking a dose of Narcan I put it under Peaches' nose to wake her, I was careful and didn't want to touch her too much. Shortly afterward she jumped up.

"Okay bitch, let me tell you something," I began talking to Peaches looking her right in the eyes. "As much as I want to cause you so much pain and kill your ass slowly, I'm not. See what I will not have is a murder charge hanging over my head. Unlike you, I'm smart, so the only people who will know I'm responsible for your death are us three right in this room. You're the reason my baby is not growing inside of me, you're the reason I went through a month of depression, and then you had the nerve to come to pick me up like everything was cool. Sadly, I didn't see a snake so close to me. You were always jealous of me Peaches, but to go this far was unnecessary. What did you get out of it? A wet pussy?" Peaches just sobbed uncontrollably; unable to say anything. She just let her head fall. "Well, now you can write your farewells bitch because you're going to hell." Taking the tape off her wrist, I handed Peaches a pen and paper so she could write her own suicide note, exactly how I wrote it on a separate sheet of paper. Soon as she took the pen she shot it across the room. "I'm not writing shit bitch! Fuck all you muthafuckaz, you gone kill me anyways," Peaches spat at me. Looking at her, I almost snapped. But I held myself together, knowing if I didn't think fast my entire plan would be ruined. "Listen Peaches, you have two options; you can write the note and live or don't write the note and die. At this point, I'm thinking hard about sparing your life because we go way

69

back. Now, if you want to walk out of this room hurt, but alive, I advise you to be smart about your decision," I tried to reason with Peaches. A twinkle of hope was shown in Peaches' eyes as she thought she had a chance at survival. Stylez picked up the pen making sure he had his gloves on and handed it back to Peaches. Looking up at me, Peaches smiled a little. "See Ang, I knew you'd come to your senses. We have been best friends before Trey came in the picture, and I'll always love you girl."

"I'll always love you too Peach," I assured her. Focusing back on the note she began writing exactly what was on the other paper beside her.

"I've made many bad choices in my life, one of them I can't live with. I was paid to lie on an innocent man. Trey Godfrey is not the man responsible for the crime. I have lost a friend because of that lie and I'm ashamed. I no longer have the desire to live anymore, afraid that I'll face retaliation for my wrongdoings. I won't be able to walk these streets without having to watch my back, I just hope everyone I've hurt can find it in their hearts to forgive me." Sincerely Peaches.

"Awe! How fucking sweet," I said while clapping my hands. "Come on Stylez let's get all this shit together," I instructed. I went to the bathroom and lathered soap on a rag, I wanted to make sure all the tape residue was off Peaches wrist. After cleaning her up a little to fit the description of suicide I untaped her. "So you are going to let me go?" Peaches asked in a cheerful voice. Stylez stood by making sure she didn't make any sudden moves. Taking the rope off from around her neck, her smile broadened until she realized Stylez was hanging the rope from a metal pole on the ceiling. Peaches stood up straight as her face twisted up knowing she was played, she reached back and slapped the shit out of me. I charged at her, but Stylez grabbed me before my fist connected with her face.

"Remember, Boss Lady, no signs of a struggle," Stylez reminded me. Looking at Peaches, I regained my composure and took a deep breath. "Well, at least before you die you got to touch the only real bitch who cared about your ass," I told her. Stylez and I stood Peaches on the chair. Trying to get the noose around her neck took about five minutes as she tried to squirm her way down. Finally, our mission was almost complete. Stylez climbed off the other chair. Before Peaches could muster up enough strength to try to release herself, I kicked the chair from under her.

"Did you think I was going to let your stupid ass live, you conniving bitch?" I taunted her as she squealed and fought for nearly 10 minutes. I watched until she yelped and tried to catch her last breath, as her eyes rolled to the back of her head, and she became limp. Walking up to her, I checked her pulse and was satisfied when her light pulse became no pulse at all. Foam leaked from her mouth and a smell, so strong, hit my nostrils. I thought I'd vomit. That's when I realized the bitch shitted on herself.

"Let's get this shit cleaned up and bounce," I told Stylez. We loaded the duffle bag and wiped down everything, making sure to leave no signs of our presence. Putting the suicide note on the bed I made sure my gloves were on, as I smirked at my intelligence. Looking back at Peaches for the last time, I shook my head in disgust. I put my scarf around my face and waited for Stylez to put his black hoodie up. We made our way down to the hotel lobby, looking like a happy couple checking out for the night. As we made our way to the exit, we both went our separate ways, disappearing like thieves in the night.

CHAPTER 15
TREY

I was sitting in my cell at the most notorious prison in history. In my time spent here, I've seen inmates beaten for nothing. If you moved wrong, talked out of turn, or tried to file a grievance, your ass was as good as dead. COs would fuck with you hoping you would say some slick shit so they could fuck you up. It was close to home which was good for Angela. In reality, they sent my young ass here, hoping I wouldn't make it out alive. With all odds against me and a murder charge hanging over my head, I knew my days were numbered.

I walked out of my cell to use the phone, it was crowded as usual. I stood in line waiting my turn. After about an hour of waiting, I made a call to Angela. She sounded like she had a million and one things to tell me, but our time was limited. I knew my wifey, I could tell when something was on her mind. Being that the calls were recorded, she was hesitant about saying the wrong things. She said she'd visit in a couple of days, I couldn't wait to see her.

After hanging up with her, I went back to my cell to draw a picture of Angela. As I began to draw, I was immediately disturbed by officer Dickhead.

"Godfrey, get your ass together you have a visitor," he yelled. Feeling a little skeptical, I began getting myself together. I knew it wasn't Angela, visiting hours were already over. Not only that, I just hung up the phone with her. I began feeling like these mufuckaz was about to take me somewhere and fuck my ass up.

After freshening up, my cell was opened and I was told to go to the visiting room. Making my way down to the visiting rooms, I turned at least 20 times watching my back as my heart raced.

Once inside the room, my heart calmed as I saw Rivers sitting at the table. What the fuck was my lawyer doing here I thought to myself.

"Trey, how are they treating you in here, man?" Rivers asked.

"Like a fuckin King, Rivers," I replied sarcastically.

Rivers pulled out paperwork from his briefcase and began, "I know you're probably wondering what I'm doing here." He flashed a smile. "I wanted you to know I got your court date moved up. Instead of next week, it will be on Thursday, which is two days from today." I didn't know what Rivers was getting at, so I continued to let him talk.

"Also, your witness was found in a hotel room hanging from the ceiling; She committed suicide and also left a note saying she was paid to frame you."

I knew I was trying to say something, but couldn't move my lips. I was still trying to process everything he said.

"So, this means I'm going to be a free man?"

"If everything goes as planned and the D.A. does not have any other tricks up their sleeves, you should walk out a free man" Rivers assured me.

After Ending the visit with Rivers, I didn't know what to think. How could this shit be happening, Peaches murked herself, and getting me off this murder charge didn't make sense. I knew something was up, but I guess I had to wait until these gates opened to find out who I owed the $100,000 to.

As I went back to E block, one of the inmates who goes by D, called me into the dayroom, "Yo Trey, yo ass on the news" he said pointing to the TV. Watching the news I saw my face on the screen. The news headline read, **"Witness commits suicide and left a note admitting to**

wrongfully accusing well-known drug lord Trey Godfrey of murder."

The dayroom erupted with cheers as all the inmates shook my hand and showed love. I was still trying to figure all this shit out, but I didn't let it show. I took all the congratulations and all the love and let it sink in. I couldn't believe I was getting away with murder. Shit like this only happened on TV, but here I was; not knowing how or even why I could be a free man.

Days seemed to go by slow as hell when you're waiting on court, but today was the day I'd go before the Judge. I woke up around five in the morning, hoping all this wasn't too good to be true.

Once I was transported to the Courthouse, I sat in the holding cell for hours. Just as I began to feel a little uneasy, the court officer unlocked the cell. "Godfrey let's go, I'll be taking you up now," the officer said as he handcuffed me and escorted me to the courtroom. As I entered the courtroom I saw Angela looking beautiful as ever, as well as my Moms, and some dude sitting next to Angela with a twisted smirk on his face. I swear I wanted to hop over the benches and beat the shit out of homeboy. I kept my composure because I knew my wifey wouldn't disrespect me like that. Court began and I swear my palms were sweating something bad. My lawyer whispered in my ear as he guaranteed that I'll be released today. After waiting an additional twenty minutes the Judge came out. The D.A. and Rivers went back and forth for about fifteen minutes deliberating. Shortly after Rivers walked back over to me with a reassuring smile splattered across his face while the D.A. looked sick to his stomach.

"After reviewing all information pertaining to Mr. Godfrey's case as well as a deceased witness statement, the courts will release Trey Godfrey immediately from Rikers Island Correctional Facility." The judge banged his gavel and concluded with, "this court is adjourned." I didnt know what the hell to do, I was ready to get the fuck out of there. I been locked down for 17 months and finally, I was a free man. As I stood up, I felt like I was being watched. Glancing throughout the courtroom a pair of wandering eye's caught my attention, but I couldn't make out who they belonged to as the officer grabbed me and escorted me out of the courtroom. I sat in the cold ass cell once again, my thoughts all over the place. I needed to get out and get answers, I didn't like being in the dark about shit. It was time for me to get out and get back on my grind. Angela deserved more than just being a wifey to a jailhouse nigga. I was going to make her my wife and that's on my life.

EPILOGUE
ANGELA

6 months later:

*L*ife has been treating Trey and me so fabulous. A week after his release he proposed to me, and of course, I said YES! With us being newly engaged and all, we have been having sex like two wild animals. Yesterday I went for my yearly exam at the doctor and found out I'm 3 months pregnant. Trey has been hysterical ever since and made sure I ate and gained weight for our baby's sake. I thought getting Trey to warm up to Stylez would be challenging, but when he got out and started bugging about him being at his court appearance, I had to break down the events that led up to him being released. Of course, Trey flipped because I put myself in that predicament. But he had to understand I was going to ride for my man, I'd also be collecting that $100,000.

After two months of Stylez being around, Trey pulled him from being a corner boy to the leader of our west coast district. Stylez was happy his position changed and Trey was happy he could spend more time at home.

After the incident with Peaches, I was a wreck for about a month. Her face appeared in my dreams and haunted me every time I closed my eyes. Eventually, the dreams began to subside, and I would wake up like... who the fuck is Peaches?

The pain I felt began to ease and I had no remorse. I wonder if that's the feeling you get when you catch a body. Even though Trey slowed down moving weight. For some reason, he said he felt like he was being watched and wanted to make sure to take precautions. I told him it was just him being paranoid, but he told me, deep down, he felt it was more to it. Trey made sure we were good and slowly but surely he was less in the streets and more at home; trusting Stylez to take complete charge. All Trey had to do was supply and demand, and leave the rest to the corner boys.

After getting out of a nice long bath on a chilly fall day, Trey asked me to get dressed, he wanted me to ride with him. He wouldn't tell me our destination because he wanted to surprise me.

Once I got myself together in a fitted red and white sweater dress that revealed my baby bump, I decided on some black knee-high, flat-heeled boots. Trey decided to match with a red button up and white dickies with red

Timbs. We hopped in our Escalade as Trey led us to our destination. As we made several turns, Trey kept his eyes in the rearview mirror, but wouldn't say why. Everything good baby?" I asked him, "Yeah, Ang. You know I be on point," he replied assuringly. I knew when something was bothering my man, for now, I let him be. I didn't want to ruin the mood. Trey turned and looked at me as he pulled over to the side of the road, "Ang, I wanted to do this in a spot that means something to me. I don't know if you remember or not, but Maine and Duval is where I first saw you walking. I hopped out on you and asked you if I could get your number."

"Yes, baby I remember," I whispered as tears escaped my eyes. Trey pulled out a set of keys, on the key chain was a diamond "A" and a diamond "T."

"Oh, my God! What is this for Trey?" I asked hysterically. "It's for our new home, " he replied as he got out of the truck and came to my side.

Before Trey opened my door he glanced over my shoulder, for the first time in my life I saw the most uneasy expression on his face.

Trey was looking into the same eyes that he had been trying to figure out all this time. Who the eyes belonged to made him even angrier. Trey wasn't strapped, he left his gun under the driver seat. I turned and looked at what

Trey's eyes were fixed on. My heart dropped when I saw the evilness in Marvin's eyes. Before anyone could move Marvin yelled, "I told you, you can't be king forever," as he pulled out a gun and started busting off shots. Trey opened my door and grabbed me, as the shots continued. Reaching into the truck he grabbed his gun from under the seat. That's when I felt a hot sensation pierce my shoulder as I screamed in agony, the burning sensation hit me instantly. Trey turned into a lunatic after hearing me scream and returned fire with Marvin, letting off every round from his 22. The veins bulged from the side of his head, his eyes were soulless. Trey covered me, shielding me with his own body as we took off running.

We eventually made it into a nearby store as I collapsed on the floor and Trey collapsed beside me. Blood was everywhere and I panicked; knowing I was hit, holding my stomach, and silently praying for our unborn child. As I tapped Trey he didn't budge, I tried lifting him; still nothing. The store owner came to help, when he lifted Trey I screamed as I saw most of the blood came from him. I could see that Trey's body was riddled with bullets; he had used his body to protect me and our baby.

I was losing lots of blood from being shot, I tried to focus on Trey, nonetheless. My body began to shake, I gasped for air and held Trey's hand. Taking another deep breath, my eyes began to roll, I had no control of my body, it began to give up and so did I. I knew it was selfish, but if I couldn't be a mother and have Trey with me, I didn't want to fight to live. I was the true definition of a jailhouse wifey; not married but I played the position of a wifey to a man in and out of jail. Before being consumed by the darkness I managed to say, "I LOVE YOU TREY." Those were the last words I said before my body went stiff.

Made in United States
Orlando, FL
20 April 2024

45954189R00061